A. A. MILNE

POEMS FROM
WHEN WE WERE VERY YOUNG

Selected with pictures by
ROSEMARY WELLS

Norton Young Readers
An Imprint of W. W. Norton & Company
Independent Publishers Since 1923

For Simon, my wonderful editor,
and Ann Bobco, who designed this book with great élan.

Copyright © 2021 by Rosemary Wells · All rights reserved · Printed in China · First Edition · For information about permission to reproduce selections from this book, write to Permissions, W. W. Norton & Company, Inc., 500 Fifth Avenue, New York, NY 10110 · For information about special discounts for bulk purchases, please contact W. W. Norton Special Sales at specialsales@wwnorton.com or 800-233-4830 · Manufacturing by Toppan Leefung · Book design by Ann Bobco · Production manager: Julia Druskin · Library of Congress Cataloging-in-Publication Data · Names: Milne, A. A. (Alan Alexander), 1882–1956, author. | Wells, Rosemary, compiler, illustrator. · Title: Poems from when we were very young / A. A. Milne ; selected with pictures by Rosemary Wells. · Other titles: When we were very young · Description: First edition. | New York : Norton Young Readers, [2021] | Audience: Ages 6–8 | Identifiers: LCCN 2021021163 | ISBN 9781324016533 (hardcover) | ISBN 9781324016540 (epub) · Subjects: LCSH: Children's poetry, English. | CYAC: English poetry. | LCGFT: Poetry. · Classification: LCC PR6025 .I65 P54 2021 | DDC 821/.912—dc23 LC record available at https://lccn.loc.gov/2021021163 · W. W. Norton & Company, Inc., 500 Fifth Avenue, New York, N.Y. 10110 · www.wwnorton .com · W. W. Norton & Company Ltd., 15 Carlisle Street, London W1D 3BS

0   8   6   4   2   1   3   5   7   9

CONTENTS

Illustrator's Note

A HUNDRED YEARS AGO, ALAN ALEXANDER MILNE WROTE A BOOK OF poetry for his three-year-old son, Christopher. It has lasted and lived in the memory of millions of children ever since.

The poetry is as fresh and clever as the lyrics of any great Broadway musical. The verses click off the tongue and embed in the mind after one reading, like a song, never to be forgotten. Milne's poems are as much fun to read aloud as they are to be heard.

I have loved the King and his buttered bread, James James Morrison Morrison, and the visit to Buckingham Palace since I was very young, and my parents read it to me and sang it around the house, seventy-five years ago.

In a picture-book format for each, here are my favorite twelve.

HAPPINESS

John

Mackintosh

Boots

Hat

HAPPINESS

John had
Great Big
Waterproof
Boots on;

John had a
Great Big
Waterproof
Hat;

John had a
Great Big
Waterproof
Mackintosh—

And that
(Said John)
Is
That.

RICE PUDDING

Mother

Mary Jane

Father

Rice Pudding

RICE PUDDING

What is the matter with Mary Jane?
She's crying with all her might and main,
And she won't eat her dinner—rice pudding again—
What *is* the matter with Mary Jane?

What is the matter with Mary Jane?
I've promised her dolls and a daisy-chain.
And a book about animals—all in vain—
What *is* the matter with Mary Jane?

What is the matter with Mary Jane?
I've promised her sweets and a ride in the train,
And I've begged her to stop for a bit and explain—
What *is* the matter with Mary Jane?

What is the matter with Mary Jane?
She's perfectly well and she hasn't a pain,
And it's lovely rice pudding for dinner again!—
What *is* the matter with Mary Jane?

DISOBEDIENCE

Mother

James

King

DISOBEDIENCE

James James
Morrison Morrison
Weatherby George Dupree
Took great
Care of his Mother,
Though he was only three.
James James
Said to his Mother,
"Mother," he said, said he:

"You must never go down to the end of the town,

if you don't go down with me."

James James
Morrison's Mother
Put on a golden gown,

James James
Morrison's Mother
Drove to the end of the town.
James James
Morrison's Mother
Said to herself, said she:

"I can get right down to the end of the town

and be back in time for tea."

King John
Put up a notice,

James James
Morrison Morrison
(Commonly known as Jim)
Told his
Other relations
Not to go blaming *him*.
James James
Said to his Mother,
"Mother," he said, said he:

"You must *never* go down to the end of the town without consulting me."

James James
Morrison's mother
Hasn't been heard of since.
King John
Said he was sorry,
So did the Queen and Prince.
King John
(Somebody told me)
Said to a man he knew:

"If people go down to the end of the town,

well, what can *anyone* do?"

LINES AND SQUARES

Me

LINES AND SQUARES

Whenever I walk in a London street,

I'm ever so careful to watch my feet;

    And I keep in the squares,

    And the masses of bears,

Who wait at the corners all ready to eat

The sillies who tread on the lines of the street,

    Go back to their lairs,

And I say to them, "Bears,
Just look how I'm walking in all of the squares!"

And the little bears growl to each other, "He's mine,
As soon as he's silly and steps on a line."

And some of the bigger bears try to pretend
That they came round the corner to look for a friend;

And they try to pretend that nobody cares
Whether you walk on the lines or squares.

But only the sillies believe their talk;
It's ever so portant how you walk.

And it's ever so jolly to call out, "Bears,

Bye, Bye, Bears!

LONDON TRANSPORT

INDEPENDENCE

Father

Kitten

Mother

INDEPENDENCE

I never did,
I never did,
I never *did* like
   "Now take care, dear!"

I never did,
I never did,
I never *did* want
   "Hold-my-hand";

I never did,
I never did,
I never *did* think much of
   "Not up there, dear!"

It's no good saying it. They don't understand.

HALFWAY DOWN

Mousie

HALFWAY DOWN

Halfway down the stairs
Is a stair
Where I sit.
There isn't any
Other stair
Quite like
It.
I'm not at the bottom,
I'm not at the top;
So this is the stair
Where
I always
Stop.

Halfway up the stairs
Isn't up,
And isn't down.
It isn't in the nursery,
It isn't in the town.

And all sorts of funny thoughts
Run round my head:
"It isn't really
Anywhere!
It's somewhere else
Instead!"

THE THREE FOXES

Fox 1

Fox 2

Fox 3

THE THREE FOXES

Once upon a time there were three little foxes
Who didn't wear stockings, and they didn't wear sockses,
But they all had handkerchiefs to blow their noses,
And they kept their handkerchiefs in cardboard boxes.

They lived in the forest in three little houses,
And they didn't wear coats, and they didn't wear trousies.
They ran through the woods on their little bare tootsies,
And they played "Touch last" with a family of mouses.

They went to a Fair, and they all won prizes—
Three plum-puddingses and three mince-pieses.
They rode on elephants and swang on swingses.
And hit three coco-nuts at coco-nut shieses.

That's all that I know of the three little foxes
Who kept their handkerchiefs in cardboard boxes.
They lived in the forest in three little houses,
But they didn't wear coats and they didn't wear trousies,
And they didn't wear stockings and they didn't wear sockses.

THE KING'S BREAKFAST

The Dairymaid

The King

The Queen

The Alderney

Butter

Marmalade

The King asked
The Queen, and

The Queen asked
The Dairymaid:
"Could we have some butter for
The Royal slice of bread?"

The Queen asked
The Dairymaid,
The Dairymaid
Said, "Certainly,
I'll go and tell
The cow
Now
Before she goes to bed."

The Dairymaid
She curtsied,
And went and told
The Alderney:

"Don't forget the butter for
The Royal slice of bread."

The Alderney
Said sleepily:
"You'd better tell
His Majesty
That many people nowadays
Like marmalade
Instead."

The Dairymaid
Said, "Fancy!"
And went to
Her Majesty.

She curtsied to the Queen, and
She turned a little red:
"Excuse me,
Your Majesty,
For taking of
The liberty,
But marmalade is tasty, if
It's very
Thickly
Spread."

The Queen said
"Oh!"
And went to
His Majesty:

"Talking of the butter for
The Royal slice of bread,
Many people
Think that
Marmalade
Is nicer.
Would you like to try a little
Marmalade
Instead?"

The King said,
"Bother!"
And then he said,
"Oh, deary me!"

The King sobbed, "Oh, deary me!"
And went back to bed.
"Nobody,"
He whimpered,
"Could call me
A fussy man;
I *only* want
A little bit
Of butter for
My bread!"

The Queen said,
"There, there!"
And went to
The Dairymaid.

The Dairymaid
Said, "There, there!"
And went to the shed.

The cow said,
"There, there!
I didn't really
Mean it;

Here's milk for his porringer
And butter for his bread."

The Queen took
The butter
And brought it to
His Majesty;

The King said,
"Butter, eh?"
And bounced out of bed.

"Nobody," he said,
    As he kissed her
    Tenderly,
"Nobody," he said,
    As he slid down
    The banisters,
"Nobody,
    My darling,
    Could call me
    A fussy man—
    BUT
"I do like a little bit of butter to my bread!"

PUPPY AND I

Puppy

I

PUPPY AND I

I met a Horse as I went walking;
We got talking,
Horse and I.
"Where are you going to, Horse, to-day?"
(I said to the Horse as he went by).
"Down to the village to get some hay.
Will you come with me?" "No, not I."

I met some Rabbits as I went walking;
We got talking,
Rabbits and I.
"Where are you going in your brown fur coats?"
(I said to the Rabbits as they went by).
"Down to the village to get some oats.
Will you come with us?" "No, not I."

I met a Puppy as I went walking;
We got talking,
Puppy and I.
"Where are you going this nice fine day?"
 (I said to the Puppy as he went by).
"Up in the hills to roll and play."
"*I'll* come with you, Puppy," said I.

BUCKINGHAM PALACE

Christopher Robin

Alice

BUCKINGHAM PALACE

They're changing guard at Buckingham Palace—
Christopher Robin went down with Alice.
Alice is marrying one of the guard.
"A soldier's life is terrible hard,"
                              Says Alice.

They're changing guard at Buckingham Palace—
Christopher Robin went down with Alice.
We saw a guard in a sentry-box.
"One of the sergeants looks after their socks,"
                                            Says Alice.

They're changing guard at Buckingham Palace—
Christopher Robin went down with Alice.
They've great big parties inside the grounds.
"I wouldn't be King for a hundred pounds,"

Says Alice.

They're changing guard at Buckingham Palace—
Christopher Robin went down with Alice.
A face looked out, but it wasn't the King's.
"He's much too busy a-signing things,"

Says Alice.

They're changing guard at Buckingham Palace—
Christopher Robin went down with Alice.

"Do you think the King knows all about *me*?"
"Sure to, dear, but it's time for tea,"
Says Alice.

JONATHAN JO

Jonathan Jo

JONATHAN JO

Jonathan Jo
Has a mouth like an "O"
And a wheelbarrow full of surprises;
If you ask for a bat,
Or for something like that,
He has got it, whatever the size is.

If you're wanting a ball,
It's no trouble at all;
Why, the more that you ask for, the merrier—
Like a hoop and a top,
And a watch that won't stop,
And some sweets, and an Aberdeen terrier.

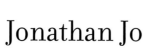

Jonathan Jo
Has a mouth like an "O"
But this is what makes him so funny:
If you give him a smile,
Only once in a while,
Then he never expects any money!

THE THIRD CHAIR

(NURSERY CHAIRS)

Sailor

I

THE THIRD CHAIR

(NURSERY CHAIRS)

When I am in my ship, I see
   The other ships go sailing by.
A sailor leans and calls to me
   As his ship goes sailing by.
Across the sea he leans to me,
   Above the winds I hear him cry:
"Is this the way to Round-the-World?"
   He calls as he goes by.

OLD-FASHIONED WORDS

There are some words in these poems that children may not know. Here are a few of them:

"Happiness"

Mackintosh
A raincoat.

"Disobedience"

Put up a notice
A notice is a big sign or advertisement.
Shillings
English money. Twenty shillings in a pound.

"Halfway Down"

Nursery
A young child's bedroom.

"The Three Foxes"

Handkerchiefs
What people used to blow their noses before they had throwaway tissues.
Trousies
Trousers, pants.
Touch last
A game of tag.
Sheises
A shie (or shy) is a booth where you throw a ball to try to knock something down and win a prize.

"The King's Breakfast"

Dairymaid
A person who takes care of the milk and butter from the cows.
Curtsied
A curtsy is a way for girls to show respect by bending their knees.
Alderney
A kind of cow who gives very good milk.
Marmalade
Orange jam.
Porringer
A bowl for porridge (which is what the English call oatmeal).

"Puppy and I"

Oats
A grain used to make oatmeal. Rabbits love to eat oats.

"Buckingham Palace"

Looks after their socks
This means the sergeant does the soldiers' laundry, including the socks.
A hundred pounds
That's English money. A pound instead of a dollar.
Time for tea
Tea is what the English often call suppertime. It's a meal.